GARFIELD'S NIGHT BEFORE CHRISTMAS

First reprint by Ravette Books Limited 1989

Printed and bound for Ravette Books Limited, 3 Glenside Estate, Star Road, Partridge Green, Horsham, West Sussex RH13 8RA by Purnell Book Production Limited, Paulton, Bristol. A member of BPCC plc

ISBN 1 85304 170 X

GARFIELD'S
NIGHT BEFORE
CHRISTMAS

KA-THUMP!

JIM DAVIS • Poem by Clement C. Moore

RAVETTE BOOKS

'Twas the night before Christmas, when all through the house
Not a creature was stirring, not even a mouse.
The stockings were hung by the chimney with care,
In hopes that St. Nicholas soon would be there.

The children were nestled all snug in their beds,
While visions of sugar-plums danced in their heads.

And Mama in her kerchief, and I in my cap,
Had just settled down for a long winter's nap,

When out on the lawn there arose such a clatter,
I sprang from my bed to see what was the matter.
Away to the window I flew like a flash,
Tore open the shutters and threw up the sash.

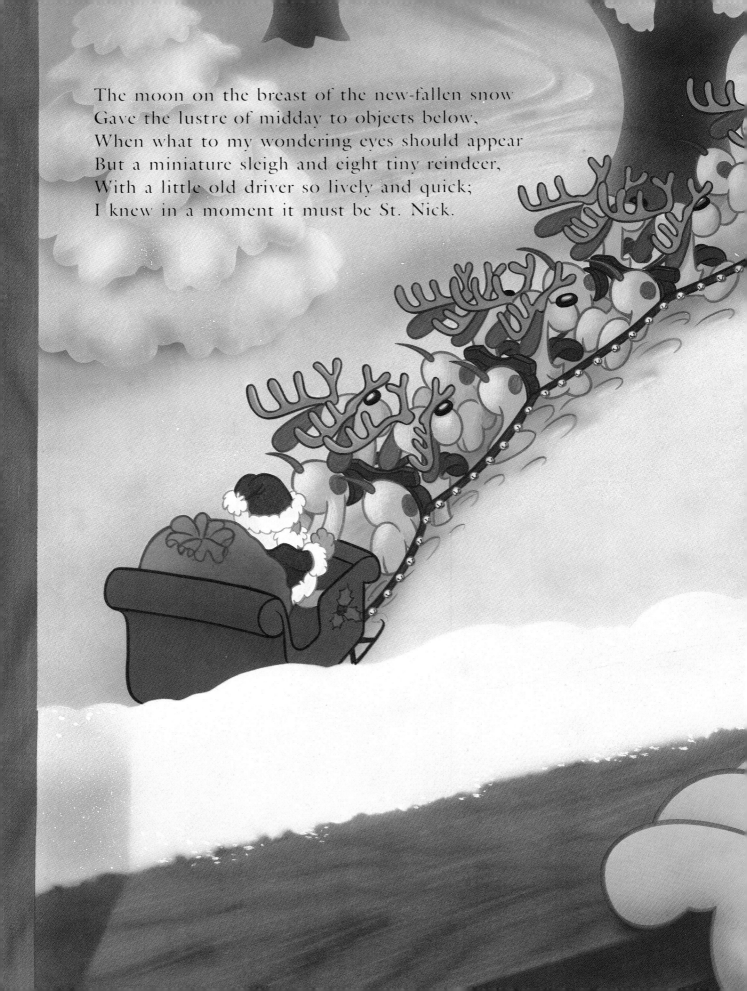

The moon on the breast of the new-fallen snow
Gave the lustre of midday to objects below,
When what to my wondering eyes should appear
But a miniature sleigh and eight tiny reindeer,
With a little old driver so lively and quick;
I knew in a moment it must be St. Nick.

More rapid than eagles his coursers they came,
And he whistled and shouted and called them by name:
"Now, Dasher! Now, Dancer! Now, Prancer and Vixen!
On, Comet! On, Cupid! On, Donner and Blitzen!
To the top of the porch! To the top of the wall!
Now, dash away, dash away, dash away all!"

As dry leaves that before the wild hurricane fly,
When they meet with an obstacle, mount to the sky,
So up to the house-top the coursers they flew
With the sleigh full of toys, and St. Nicholas, too.

And then in a twinkling I heard on the roof
The prancing and pawing of each little hoof.
As I drew in my head and was turning around,
Down the chimney St. Nicholas came with a bound.

He was dressed all in fur from his head to his foot,
And his clothes were all tarnished with ashes and soot.
A bundle of toys he had flung on his back,
And he looked like a pedlar just opening his sack.

His eyes, how they twinkled! His dimples, how merry!
His cheeks were like roses, his nose like a cherry!
His droll little mouth was drawn up like a bow,
And the beard on his chin was as white as the snow.

The stump of a pipe he held tight in his teeth,
And the smoke it encircled his head like a wreath.
He had a broad face and a little round belly
That shook when he laughed like a bowl full of jelly.

He was chubby and plump, a right jolly old elf,
And I laughed when I saw him, in spite of myself.
A wink of his eye and a twist of his head
Soon gave me to know I had nothing to dread.

He spoke not a word but went straight to his work,
And filled all the stockings...

...then turned with a jerk.
And laying his finger aside of his nose
And giving a nod, up the chimney he rose.

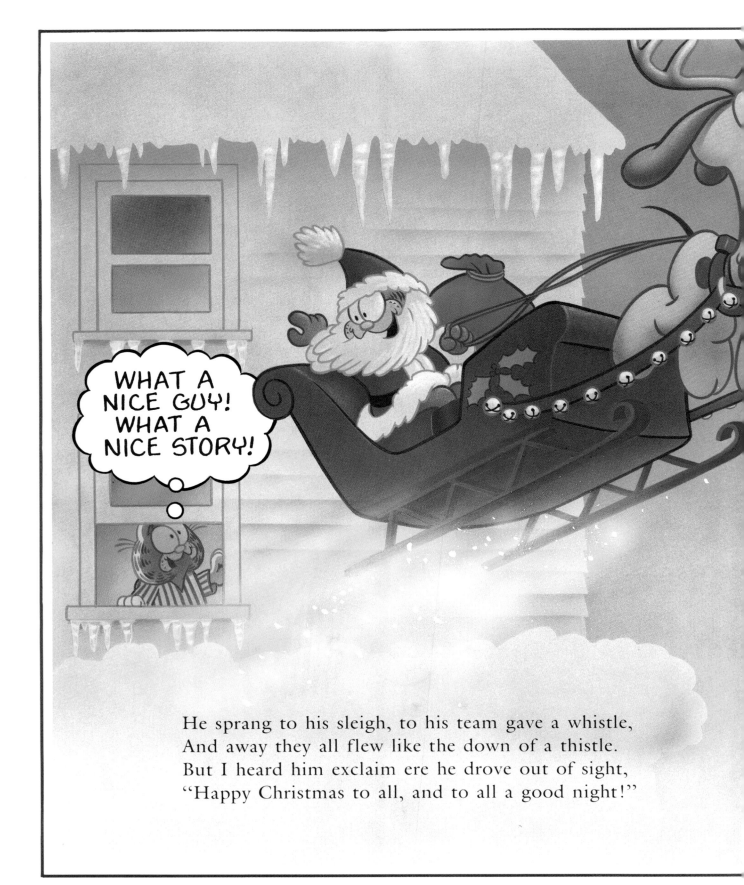

He sprang to his sleigh, to his team gave a whistle,
And away they all flew like the down of a thistle.
But I heard him exclaim ere he drove out of sight,
"Happy Christmas to all, and to all a good night!"